Aminah and A Eid Gifts

By Fawzia Gilani-Williams

Goodwordkidz

Helping you build a family of faith

"How many things do you have on your list?" asked Aisha. "Seven, but I'm going to add one more," said Aminah. "How many do you have on yours?"

"Oh eight, I think," replied Aisha.

Every Eid, Aminah and Aisha would prepare an Eid list. They would write down things that they wanted to buy. Just then Abba called the girls. It was nearly time to break the fast. The girls raced to the bathroom to make wudu.

"What did you make Abba?" asked Aisha with a look of worry on her face.

"Fruit salad, Cheeseballs and Rice with Kofta stew!" gleamed Abba, with a huge smile on his face. "Your mother is going to be impressed."

Aisha set out the glasses while Aminah set the plates and put a dish of dates at the center of the table.

A key turned in the door.

"Oooh Ammi's home!" burst Aisha running to greet her. Ammi looked very tired when she walked in through the door. She had a hard day at the office.

"*Asalaamu alaikum* everyone," greeted Ammi.

"*Wa alaikum salaam*!" chimed the girls loudly, just as if they were at school. Abba took Ammi's coat and hung it up.

"How was your day?" asked Abba.

"Very busy and very tiring," answered Ammi shaking her head. "How about yours?"

"Oh, I got off work early and picked up the girls from school," answered Abba.

"They must have liked that," smiled Ammi.

Soon the family was settled down at the table waiting for the *adhan* to be called.

"Whose turn?" asked Abba.

Aisha picked up her finger to indicate it was hers. She cleared her throat and recited the *dua*: "*Allahumma laka samtu wa a'laa rizqika aft'artu wa a'layka tawakaltu.*"

Everyone broke their fast with a date and a drink of water. Then they offered *Salat-ul-Maghrib* and returned to their meal.

"O *masha Allah*! This is so tasty!" said Ammi, looking at Abba. "Are you sure you made this by yourself?" Abba laughed.

Aminah finished first. She recited the *dua* for finishing her meal. "*Alhamdu lilahil ladhi at amana wa saqana wa ja alana minal Muslimeen.*"

6

"How was school today?" asked Ammi.

Aisha told how her class was practicing a play for the Eid presentation next week.

Aminah told how her teacher had picked her idea for Eid gifts to the community. "My class will make food trays to send to the hospital, police and fire department. We get a small tray and put candy, cookies, and cakes on it and then we wrap it up with transparent colored sheets and put a ribbon on the top. Then another group writes a card explaining what Eid-ul-Fitr is all about!"

"*Masha Allah*! That's a wonderful idea," complimented Abba.

After eating Aisha and Aminah helped clear the table.

9

"Get your homework girls," called Abba. "We have an hour before we go to mosque for *Tarawih*."

Aisha worked on her reading assignment and practiced her lines for the play. Aminah worked on her science worksheet and practiced *Sura Lail*.

After the girls had finished, Ammi asked them if they had made their Eid lists.

"Yes we did!" replied both the girls excitedly. "When will you take us shopping Ammi?" they asked.

"Tomorrow, *insha Allah*," said Ammi. "I only have to work half a day and it's also your last day of school. It'll be Eid Break, so I'll pick you up after school."

The girls were so excited, they could hardly wait.

11

The next day at school was fun. The spirit of Eid was everywhere. There were balloons decorating the corridors with crescents and stars dangling from the ceiling. Streams of glittering tinsel and beads hung along the walls. All the classrooms looked so colourful, but Sister Sara's room always looked the most festive. Inside her classroom the children were busy writing cards and arranging the Eid Trays. Aminah kept looking at her watch. She couldn't wait to go shopping.

"Why do you keep looking at your watch?" asked Fahar, who was always very inquisitive.

"My mom's going to take us to buy Eid presents today," gleamed Aminah, her eyes wide open. "Oh! That's nice! What are you going to buy for yourself?" questioned Fahar.

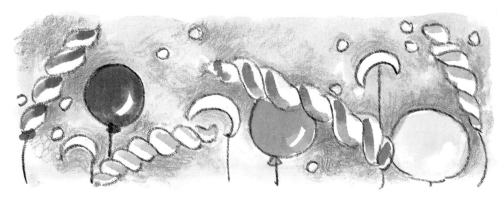

13

"Well we're not exactly..." began Aminah. But just then Sister Sara spoke, "Children please concentrate on the tasks you are doing". Both Aminah and Fahar stopped talking immediately.

Finally the school bell signaled the end of the day. Aminah was the first to be ready. *"Mashallah* Aminah!" said Sister Sara. "Excellent. You may be the first to leave."

"Jazak Allahu Khairan!" thanked Aminah.

"Barak Allah fi kum!" returned Sister Sara.

Aminah hurried to Aisha's class. Aisha had been dismissed and was standing by her locker. "Come on hurry up," said Aminah. "Here, give me your bag, I'll carry it," she offered, hoping to hurry Aisha along.

The girls finally sat in the car and Ammi drove them to the shopping centre. The girls had so much fun picking and choosing the things on their Eid list. They picked out clothes, stationary, and toys.

Soon it would be time to break the fast. "Let's go to Ali Baba's Take-Away and get *Doner Kebabs* and sweet, ice cold *Lassee*," suggested Ammi. The girls thought it was a wonderful idea. On the ride home the smell of the *Doner Kebabs* filled the car. "Oh! I can hardly wait!" exclaimed Aisha.

Finally they got home. Abba was reading Quran. "Did you get everything?" he asked.

"Yes *alhamdulilah*," they answered. "For *iftar*, we also got *Doner Kebabs* and *Lassee* too!" said Aminah.

Later in the evening after the *iftar*, Ammi got some hot chocolate for the girls while Abba told them the story of Prophet Job ﷺ.

"Tomorrow is Wednesday and there's no school," said Ammi. "So you can sort through your Eid gifts tomorrow."

"According to the Observatory, *inshallah*, Eid will be on Friday," announced Abba.

"*Allahu Akbar*! That's so wonderful!" shouted the girls, linking their arms in delight and skipping in circles.

"Okay girls" interrupted Abba, "Let's get ready for *Tarawih*."

That night Aisha dreamed about the shopping trip and about Eid. She was awoken by the alarm clock. It was time for *suhoor*.

She could hear Amma's soft voice reciting the Qur'an. She jumped up hoping to get to the bathroom before Aminah, to make *wudu*. But Aminah was already awake and sitting on her prayer mat.

After *suhoor* and the *Fajr* prayer the girls went back to bed.

In a few hours they were awake again. Abba insisted they make their beds before they attended to the Eid presents.

"I'll go into the garage and get you two boxes while you organize your rooms," he said.

The girls ran to tidy their rooms and hurried back excitedly. "Here are the boxes!" called Abba. "Let's get our Eid list," advised Aminah. "Just so that we don't mix up the presents."

Ammi and Abba always taught the girls to give happiness to others, especially at Eid. So every Eid the girls would send an Eid box to someone who was feeling sad. This Eid, Aminah was preparing a box for Muslimah, whose mother had been sick for many months and Aisha was preparing a box for Hamza, whose father had lost his job. The girls filled the boxes with Eid clothes, money, toys and other gifts. Abba helped girls wrap the boxes. Soon the boxes were ready to be taken to the post office.

"Allah wants us to help the poor and needy. When we help others, Allah helps us!" Abba and Ammi would say.

On Friday evening, Muslimah, phoned Aisha's home.

"Eid Mubarak! I got the box!" she exclaimed, "I never had such pretty Eid clothes and wonderful gifts. May Allah bless you all for thinking of me and making this such a lovely Eid."

Hamza also called. He was so happy. Hamza's mother thanked Ammi saying, "Your family made our Eid into such a joyful day!"

Abba and Ammi would always answer, "Alhamdulilah, all praise and thanks be to Allah who makes all things possible."